CYRUS THE VIRUS

D. J. CHAKRABORTY

To order additional copies of this book, contact:
Xlibris
844-714-8691
www.Xlibris.com
Orders@Xlibris.com

ISBN: Softcover   978-1-6641-5620-3
        Hardcover   978-1-6641-5621-0
        EBook   978-1-6641-5619-7

Library of Congress Control Number: 2021902364

Print information available on the last page

Rev. date: 07/07/2021

contents

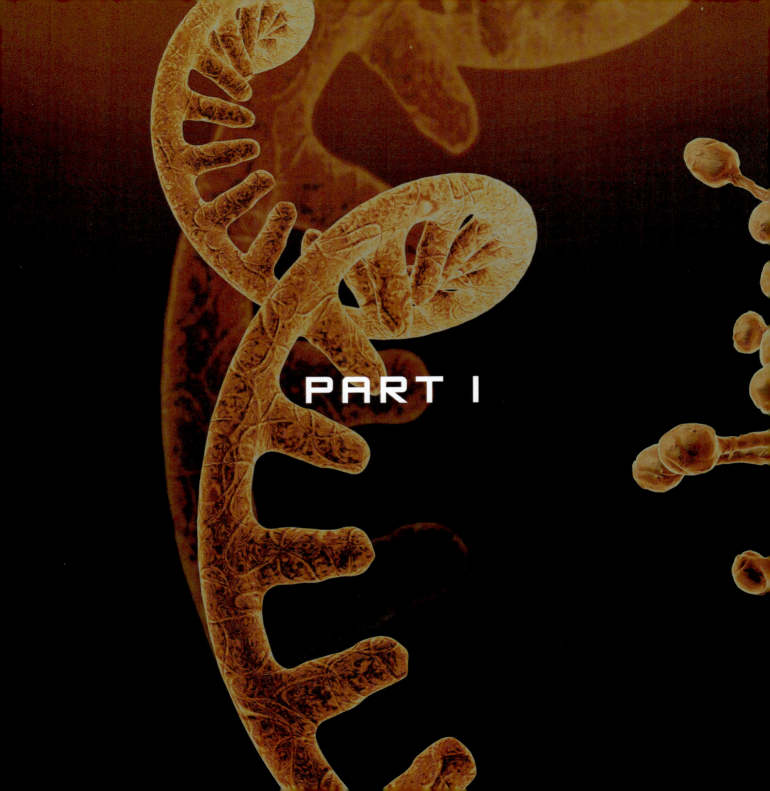

PART I

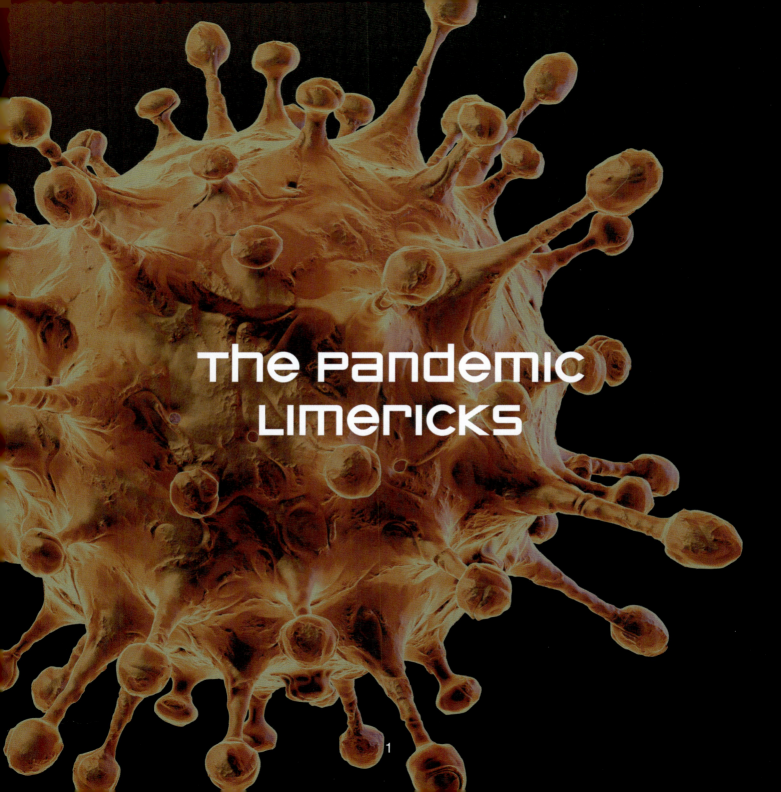

THE PANDEMIC LIMERICKS

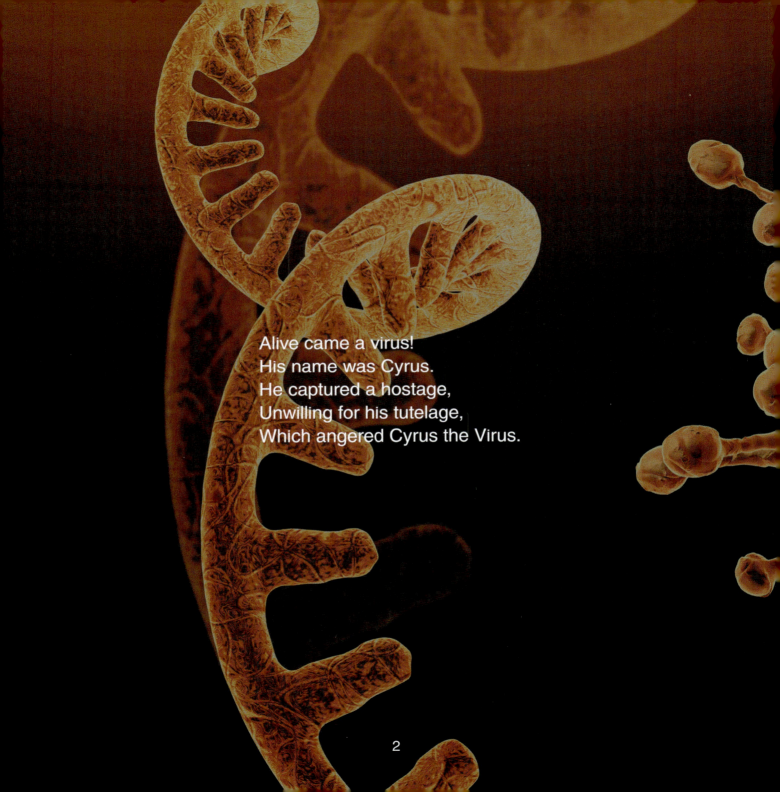

Alive came a virus!
His name was Cyrus.
He captured a hostage,
Unwilling for his tutelage,
Which angered Cyrus the Virus.

So spreads the tale of Cyrus the Virus,
His long-standing captive was growing an iris.
She lay feverish, aching for hours,
Unable to tend her lovely flowers.
Such was living under Cyrus the Virus.

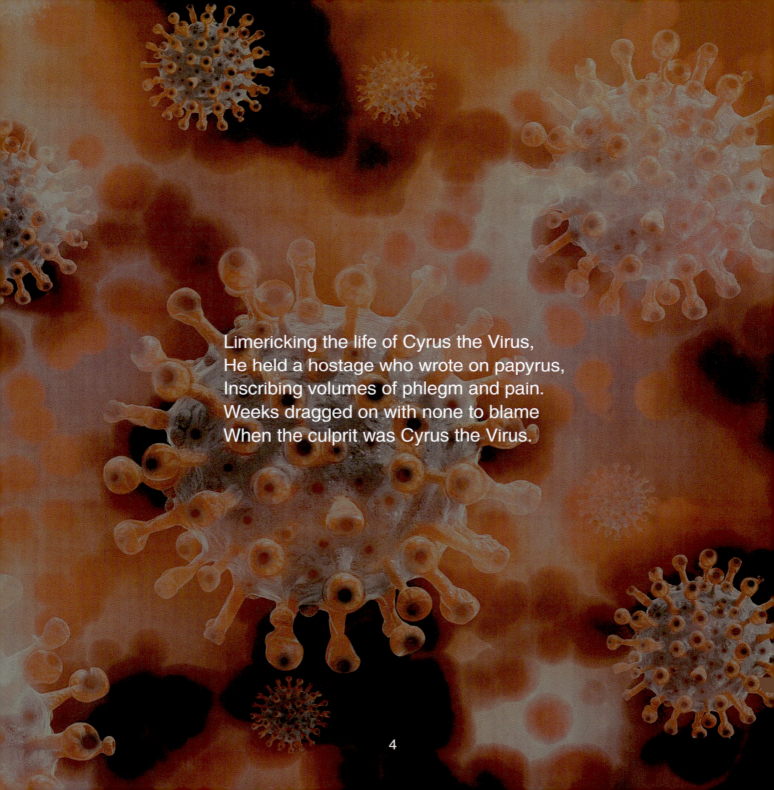

Limericking the life of Cyrus the Virus,
He held a hostage who wrote on papyrus,
Inscribing volumes of phlegm and pain.
Weeks dragged on with none to blame
When the culprit was Cyrus the Virus.

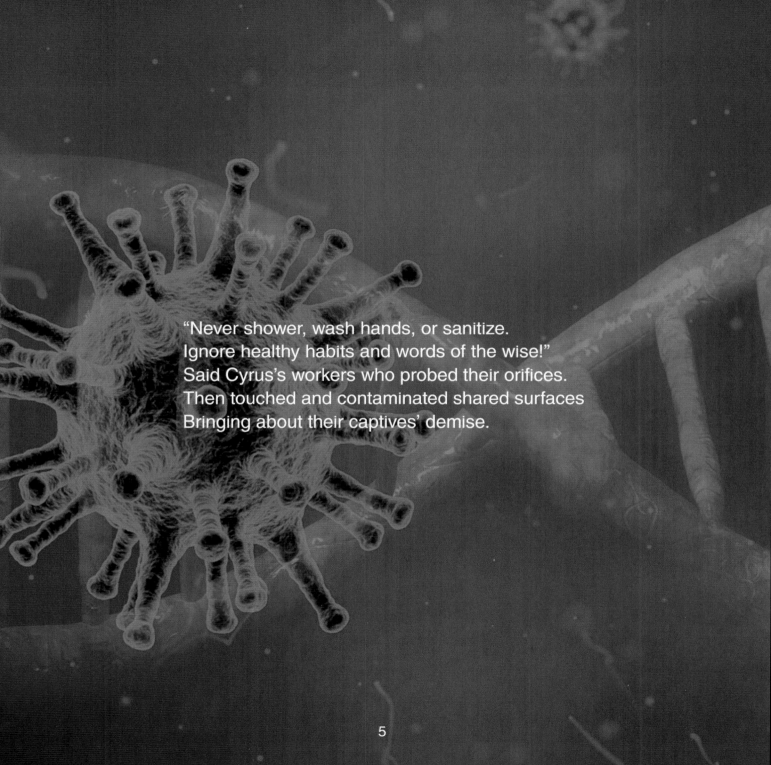

"Never shower, wash hands, or sanitize.
Ignore healthy habits and words of the wise!"
Said Cyrus's workers who probed their orifices.
Then touched and contaminated shared surfaces
Bringing about their captives' demise.

Discontented and bored with biological disease,
Cyrus the Virus still loved a cough and a sneeze.
Sent malicious warriors in software to sneak
And flummoxed the savviest computer geek,
Causing the technology to die or to freeze.

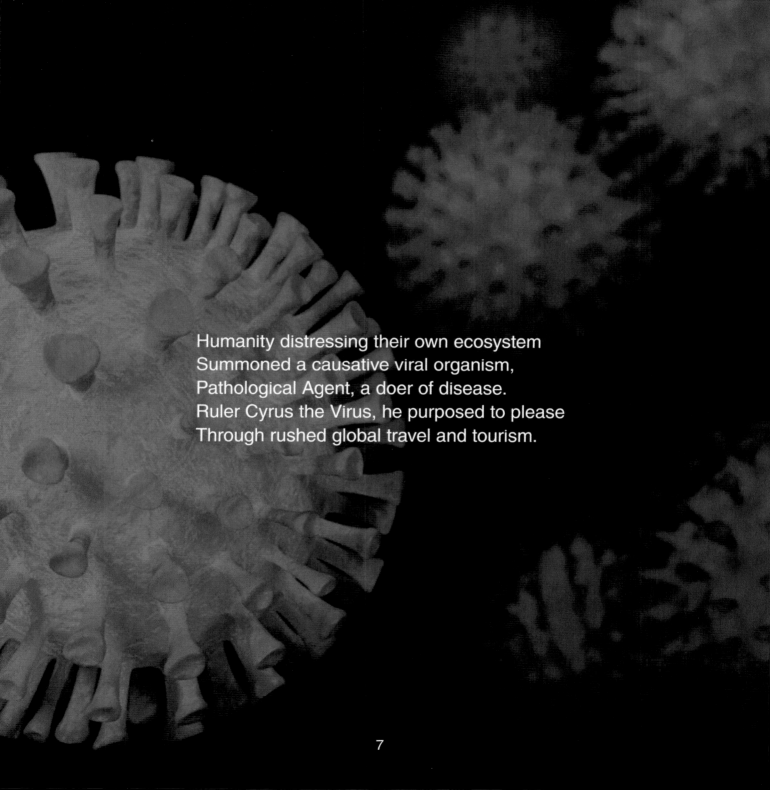

Humanity distressing their own ecosystem
Summoned a causative viral organism,
Pathological Agent, a doer of disease.
Ruler Cyrus the Virus, he purposed to please
Through rushed global travel and tourism.

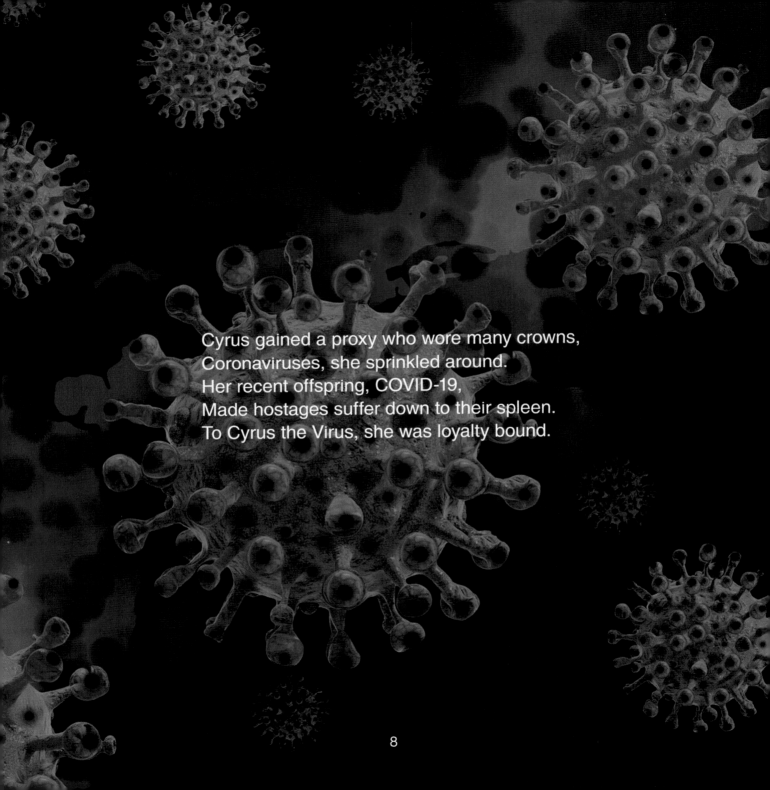

Cyrus gained a proxy who wore many crowns,
Coronaviruses, she sprinkled around.
Her recent offspring, COVID-19,
Made hostages suffer down to their spleen.
To Cyrus the Virus, she was loyalty bound.

Best defense is to wear a mask,
Although a tedious, troublesome task.
Feels uncomfortable and hard to breathe
But covers against Cyrus's viral seed.
All things considered, not much to ask.

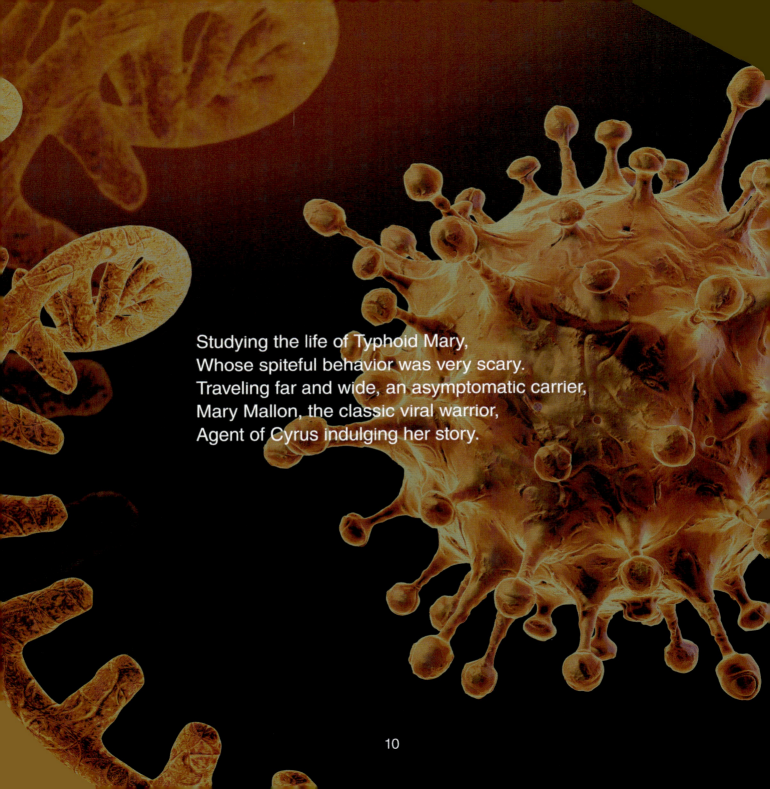

Studying the life of Typhoid Mary,
Whose spiteful behavior was very scary.
Traveling far and wide, an asymptomatic carrier,
Mary Mallon, the classic viral warrior,
Agent of Cyrus indulging her story.

Thus progresses Cyrus's humorless limerick,
Documenting 2019, '20, '21's pandemic
Feel chronic cough and short of breath?
Don't scoff, for Cyrus can bring death.
Pathological, phobic, nefarious, neurotic.

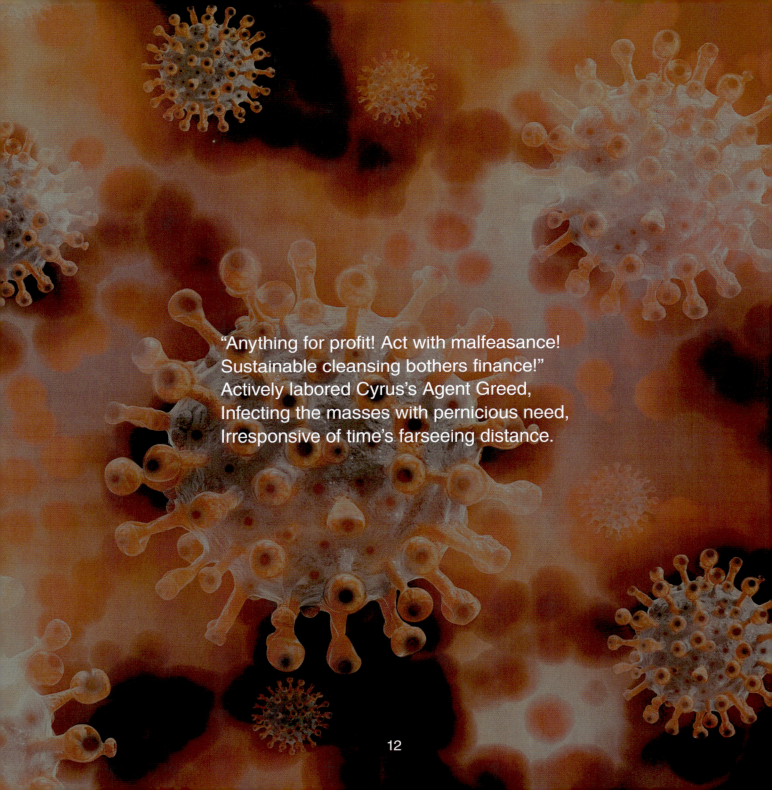

"Anything for profit! Act with malfeasance!
Sustainable cleansing bothers finance!"
Actively labored Cyrus's Agent Greed,
Infecting the masses with pernicious need,
Irresponsive of time's farseeing distance.

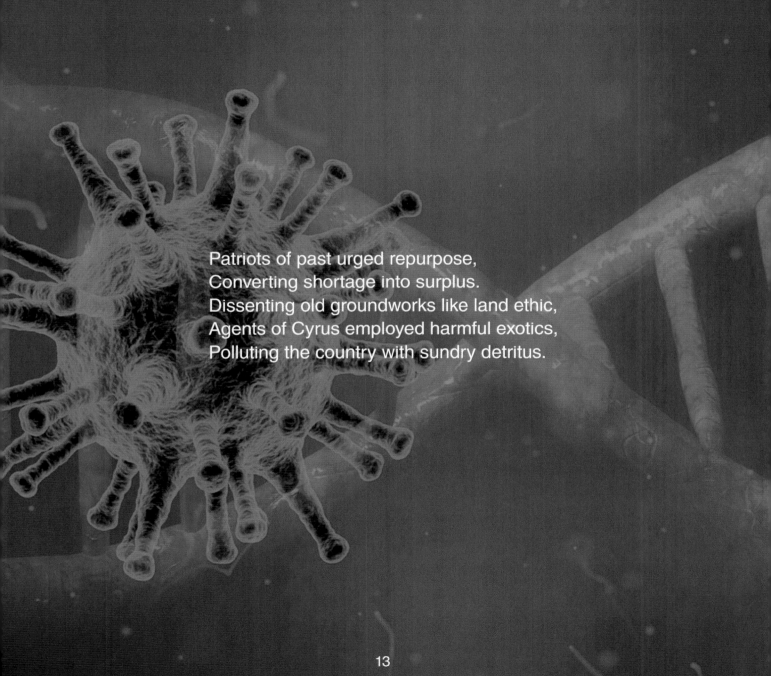

Patriots of past urged repurpose,
Converting shortage into surplus.
Dissenting old groundworks like land ethic,
Agents of Cyrus employed harmful exotics,
Polluting the country with sundry detritus.

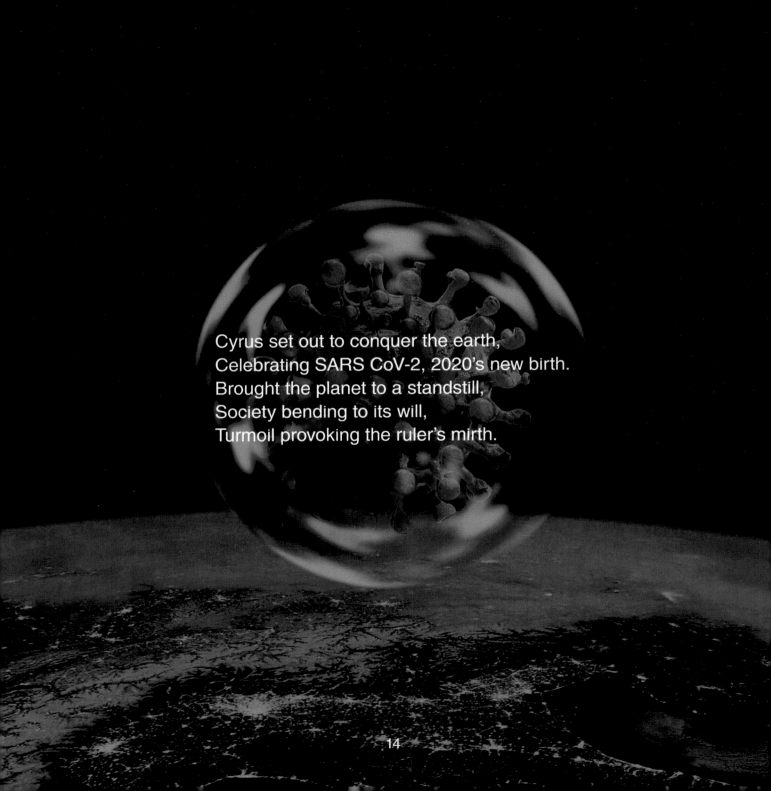

Cyrus set out to conquer the earth,
Celebrating SARS CoV-2, 2020's new birth.
Brought the planet to a standstill,
Society bending to its will,
Turmoil provoking the ruler's mirth.

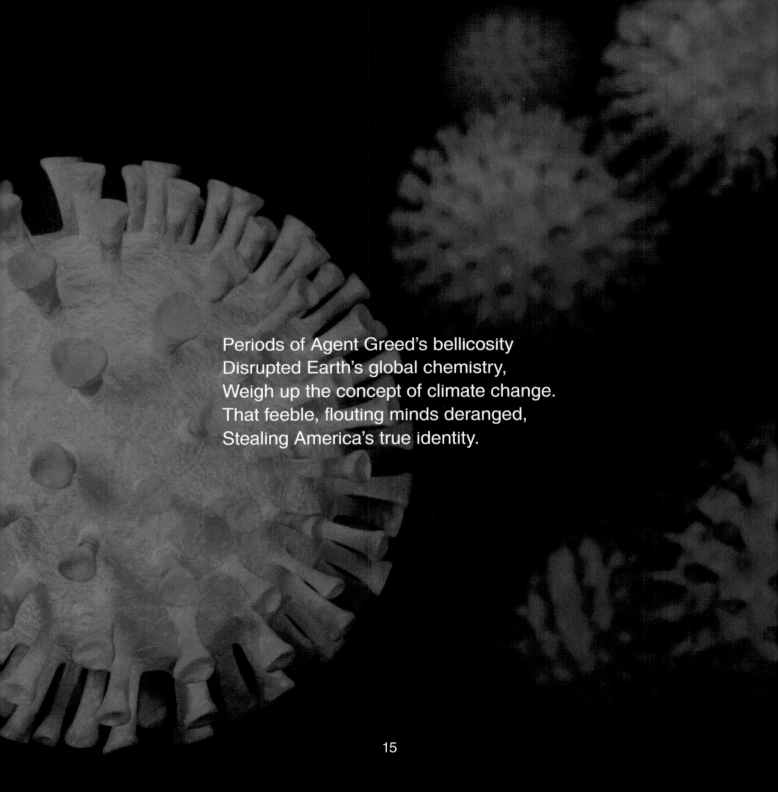

Periods of Agent Greed's bellicosity
Disrupted Earth's global chemistry,
Weigh up the concept of climate change.
That feeble, flouting minds deranged,
Stealing America's true identity.

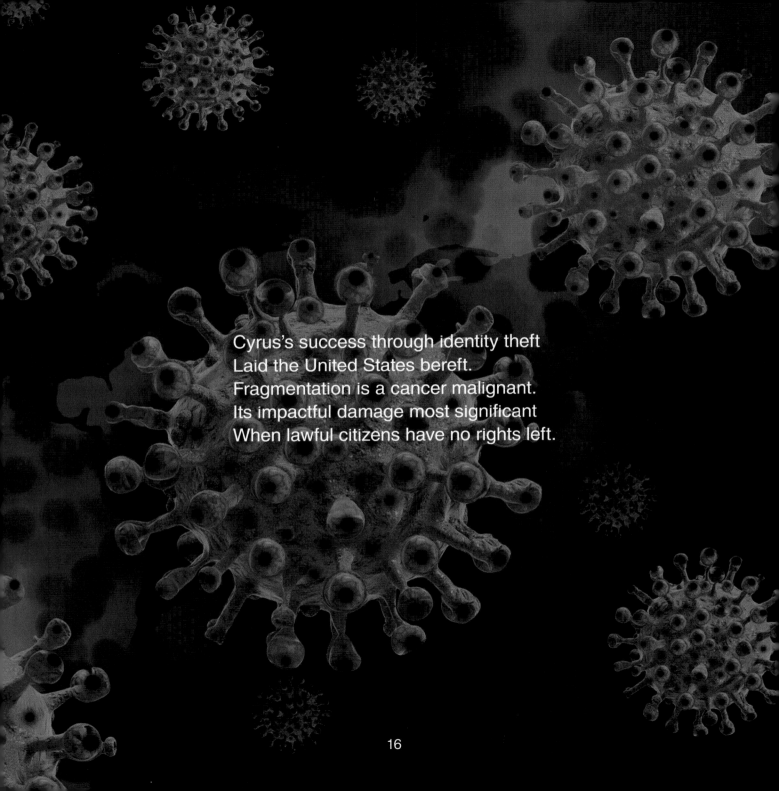

Cyrus's success through identity theft
Laid the United States bereft.
Fragmentation is a cancer malignant.
Its impactful damage most significant
When lawful citizens have no rights left.

Recall the life of Aldo Leopold,
Force of good nature, brave, and bold.
Introduced environmental stewardship,
Valuables measured by the kip,
Saving the green to recover the gold.

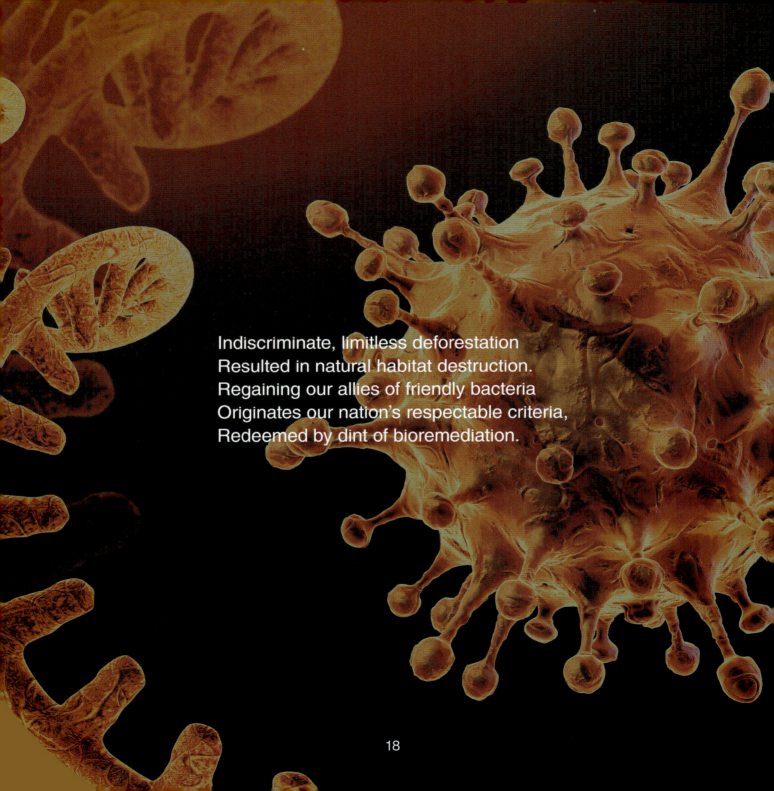

Indiscriminate, limitless deforestation
Resulted in natural habitat destruction.
Regaining our allies of friendly bacteria
Originates our nation's respectable criteria,
Redeemed by dint of bioremediation.

American invention and innovation,
Cyrus the Virus has no invitation.
Stopped at the intelligent disinfection door
And banned by Microban- 24,
Bunged through STEAMing[1] imagination.

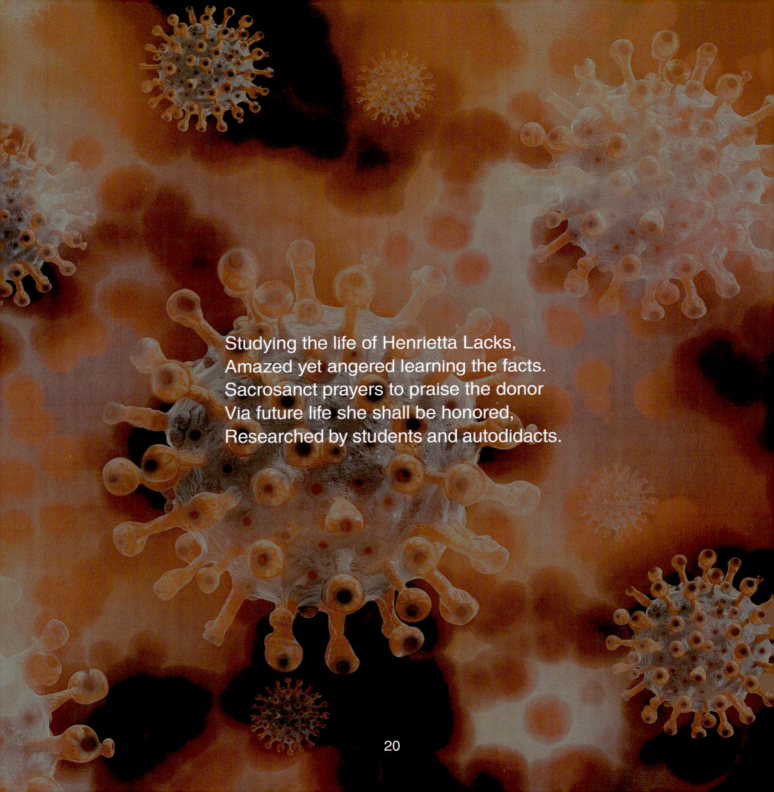

Studying the life of Henrietta Lacks,
Amazed yet angered learning the facts.
Sacrosanct prayers to praise the donor
Via future life she shall be honored,
Researched by students and autodidacts.

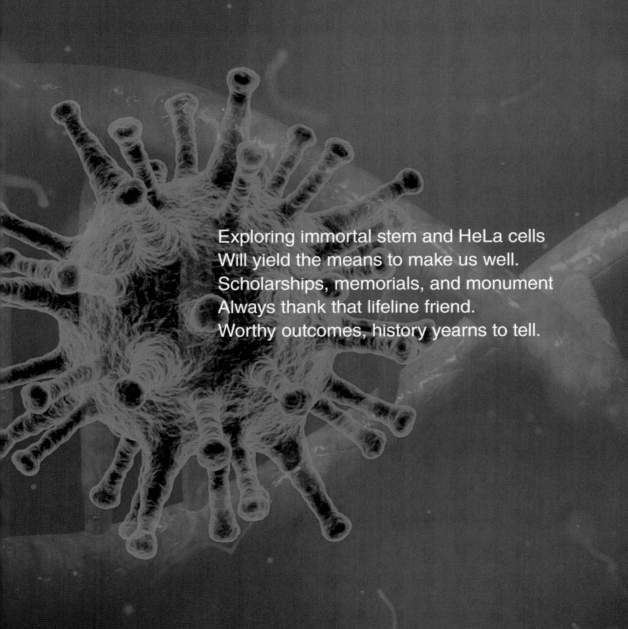

Exploring immortal stem and HeLa cells
Will yield the means to make us well.
Scholarships, memorials, and monument
Always thank that lifeline friend.
Worthy outcomes, history yearns to tell.

God already provided the best vaccine.
Fresh air, pure water, acres of green
Are the means to end this pestilence.
Root of disorder, hoarders, and violence,
Practice to sustain and keep Earth clean.

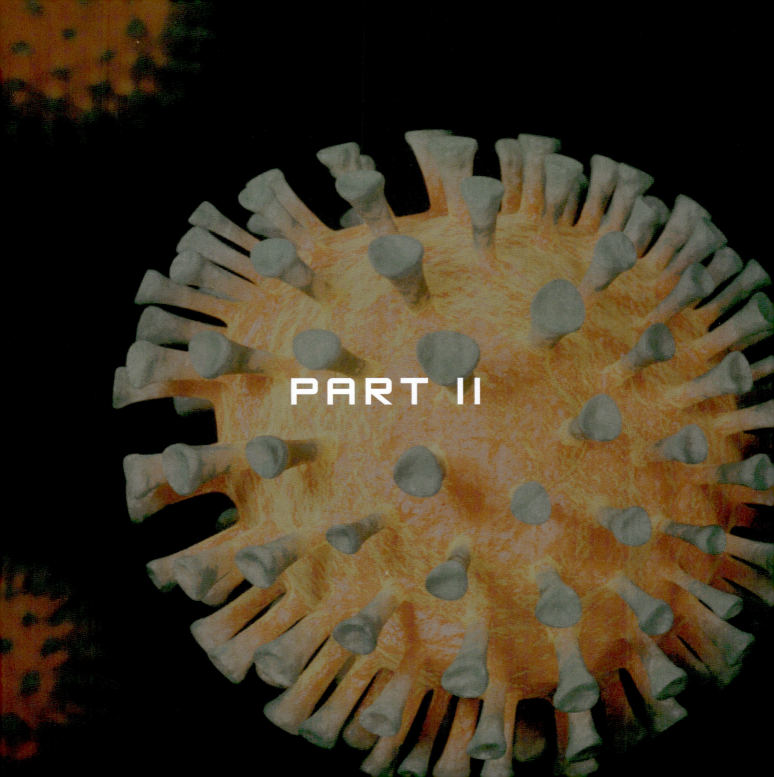

what? what? what?

Infectious agents of miniscule size, viruses only replicate inside the living cells of other life forms. Replication happens because the virus begins its life by raiding a living plant or animal cell and turning it into a biological copy machine. Remember that human beings, *Homo sapiens*, are also animals! Any living entity must have the ability to exist independently. Therefore, this microbiological oddity is not considered alive until it enters a living host body and begins to make replicas of itself.

Germ is the general term for microbes or microorganisms. There are four types of such microbiological organisms or germs. Bacteria, fungi, and protists are also microorganisms like viruses, but unlike viruses, they are actual life forms. Parasites are an unusual category; although requiring a host to survive, they are still plants like the mistletoe or animals like vampire bats or fungi like mildew. Most germs and parasites are not harmful to healthy human beings.

Bacteria, fungi, protists, and parasites can also be helpful. For example, mistletoe is used to treat cancer, edible mushrooms are delicious fungi, and *Lactobacillus acidophilus* is a type of friendly bacteria. One-celled protists perform numerous functions; seaweed is an edible protist, and carrageenan is used to make ice cream and pudding. Protists produce half of Earth's oxygen through photosynthesis. Others decompose and recycle nutrients in soil, and more are used to create medicines, cosmetics, and even plastic.

Viruses are always harmful and can kill even the healthiest creatures. Any infected host can release viral material by sneezing, coughing, expectorating, and then contacting a surface or facility. The extant virus can lay dormant but cannot make copies of itself on non-living objects, such as clothes, toilets, desktops, or computer keyboards. Weird and waiting, a latent virus comes alive when the next corporeal host touches the contaminated object. Upon being born again, the virus resumes its old system of making copies of itself.

The virus's other talent is the ability to mutate from host to host or *hostage* to *hostage*. Therefore, many viral diseases like the common cold and influenza, as well as coronavirus (COVID-19) have no cure and can be deadly because they constantly change to dominate their hostages and fight off medications. Each mutant virus brings a unique type of suffering to each unique hostage. The combined properties of replication, latency, and mutation make viruses deadly.

Isaac Newton's third law of motion states that every action has an equal and opposite reaction. The concept can be applied to more than physics. Knowing the harmful properties of viruses, human beings can think of ways to counteract them to avoid being captured, hence the logic behind cleaning and sanitizing surfaces and facilities, such as clothes, toys, bathrooms, and kitchens. Furthermore, always wash hands or shower if necessary upon contacting certain surfaces and facilities.

For centuries, many people were captured and had suffered from mutants of the influenza virus. Each viral mutation caused its numerous hostages to suffer with high, persistent fever and chills. Excessive phlegm brought sore throats, coughing, and blocked nasal passages. Severe headaches, body aches, breathing difficulty, and fatigue further plagued the unfortunate hostages. The evil ordeal was and still is able to prolong for one week to six weeks—the average was two to three weeks. COVID-19 is a game changer.

Technology, although non-biological, is not immune to viruses. This phenomenon is called a computer virus. The modus operandi of the computer virus is a *mal*icious soft*ware* program, *malware* for short. Malware sneaks into a host computer often through electronic mail or appearing as a legitimate website. Once clicked by a naive, unsuspecting user, the computer virus replicates itself by altering the technological hostage's program with its own code. Unfortunately, a computer virus can destroy/kill the hard drive, and many computers fail to recover. Hopefully, valuable data was backed up; otherwise, it is lost/dead.

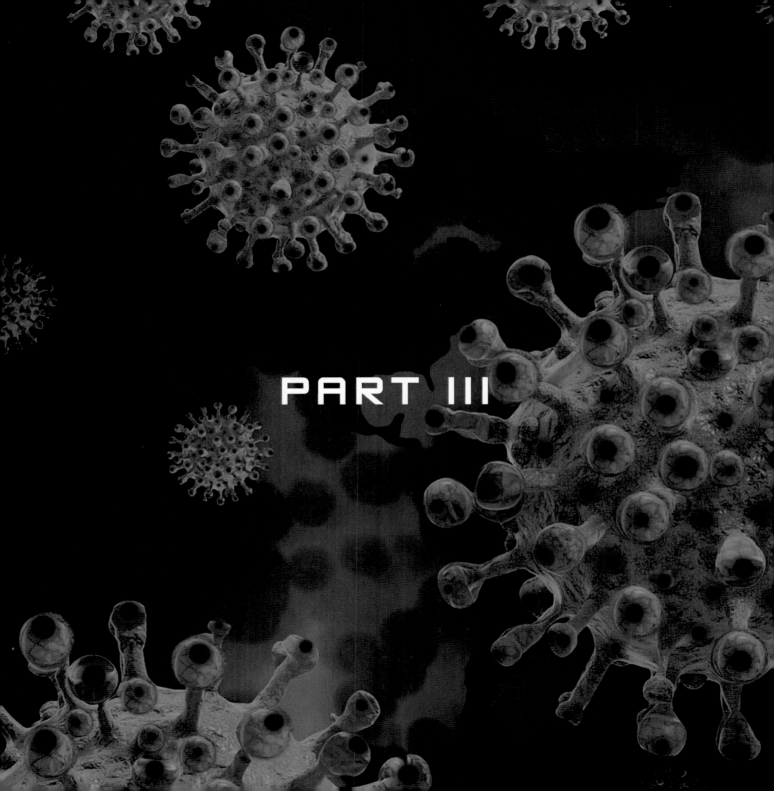

PART III

where and when?

Modern viruses like COVID-19 find origins from causative organisms which have existed on Earth for millennia. Populations of past societies were protected from contacting such organisms by inviolate local vegetation housing native flora and fauna. Those ecosystems in their backyards served humanity faithfully and voluntarily as air purifiers, air conditioners, snack bars, beauty salons, laboratories, theaters, playgrounds, and the first line of defense against dreadful diseases, like the coronavirus. Today beneficial flora and fauna are caught in the cross fire of neonicotinoid pesticides and other caustic substances. Pollinators, especially *Apis mellifera* or honeybee, are threatened due to harmful chemicals; therefore, our grandchildren may inherit a world without honey.

The American mindset is illustrated by Katharine Lee Bates's poetic lines from "America the Beautiful."[2] Most poignant and much loved are the last two lines of the second verse, *"Confirm thy soul in self-control, Thy liberty in law!"* Americans are more about mindsets than mandates, and American ideals stipulate doing right and reaching out to help those less fortunate. Good civic sense, community service, and volunteerism are indelible for good citizenship; many enjoy the camaraderie wearing masks and sanitizing their locales to help and protect fellow human beings.

The American landscape and farm were integral to creating our national identity and inspiring our Founding Fathers and were the most powerful ammunition in

---

2   For further information, please read <u>America the Beautiful</u> by Katharine Lee Bates, also learn the music by Samuel Augustus Ward, and sing the song.

winning the Revolutionary War. Encouraged by our vast arable lands, Benjamin Franklin stated that there was nothing America could not produce, therefore compelling the British to end the Stamp Tax. George Washington and John Adams would start their day with a fresh dose of oxygen by taking a morning walk or ride. Thomas Jefferson admired the scientific and economic values of the American farmstead. The logic behind summer vacation was to allow children time to help on the family farm. Our Founding Fathers' love of gardening was intertwined with politics and woven into our Constitution.

Recalling the beloved 1964 classic The Giving Tree[3] adds to the list of mutualisms between human life and green life. Equally loved, the 1971 classic The Lorax[4] warns of synnecrosis. Animals exhale carbon dioxide, and trees employ that carbon dioxide energy and express oxygen; we will not be able to breathe without plants. Anthropogenic industry, technology, and other activities exhale toxins into the atmosphere, and plants work generously to clean up after us. Hence, vegetation produces fresh air. A polluted, unsanitary environment causes natural bodily defenses to weaken; therefore, destroying vegetation means damaging human health.

Green spaces also grow fresh water through the process of transpiration. Transpiration is the evaporation of water from plant life by the process of moisture carried from the roots to the pores on the underside of leaves. There the water changes to vapor and is released into the atmosphere. Transpiration is responsible for more than ten percent (10%) of atmospheric moisture. With the increasing anthropogenic population and decreasing protective biomes,

---

3   For further information, please read The Giving Tree by Shel Silverstein.
4   For further information, please read The Lorax by Dr. Suess.

dangerous organisms like coronavirus (COVID-19 and SARS CoV-2) are gaining leverage.

The majority of such ecosystems housing indigenous vegetation and wildlife, the natural predators of harmful organisms, are vulnerable or vanished today. Human society of the twenty-first century has dismissed numerous good, healthy habits and practices in favor of bad habits and malpractices, thus allowing dangerous organisms to be released into the atmosphere, contact new victims, and spread more efficiently. Furthermore, many malpractices, which were tried and failed long ago, are rearing their ugly heads again.

Discovering the origin of the deadly coronavirus (COVID-19 and SARS CoV-2) has bewildered some of the brightest minds. There are also suspicions of viruses being created in a Chinese laboratory as weapons of bioterror. Conspiracy theories of the sort have acquired mythological proportions and appeal to the masses seeking a simple answer. Mobs of substandard brains prefer a simplistic excuse to target a common enemy to demonize and abuse, whereas intelligent individuals prefer to analyze the situation and contemplate reasonable solutions.

PART IV

Here and Now

The true origin of COVID-19 happened to be located in Wuhan, China, at a food market, not a laboratory. Although the virus manifested in China, it was not created there. COVID-19 is the natural phenomenon of bushmeat. *Bushmeat* is the term for meat from wild animals. Wild animals[5] defer greatly from their domestic counterparts. Wild animal flesh is not suitable for human consumption because it contains numerous zoonotic pathogens, which creates a vector for infectious diseases, including the current coronavirus (COVID-19 and SARS CoV-2).

Overpopulated countries such as China and India are dealing with issues such as food shortages, atmospheric pollution, increasing prices as well as declining health and resources. Meat is the most consumptive food because it requires the most resources to produce. Herds of cattle or sheep need barns for shelter, fields for grazing, and water to drink. Costly veterinary care is also necessary to prevent pests and diseases to keep the meat clean. Furthermore, expensive breeding and production techniques are required to meet customer demand.

In many parts of India, people live as vegetarians or vegans to solve this food shortage problem. China, on the other hand, turns to bushmeat. Although many avid game hunters eat their kills and laugh at disease warnings (please see list), average *Homo sapiens* adapted to suburban lifestyles, and grocery stores are vulnerable. The current pandemic illustrates how everyday people can suffer from exposure.

---

5   For further information, please read <u>Beware of Cassy</u> by D. J. Chakraborty.

The human immunodeficiency virus (HIV) originated from simian immunodeficiency virus (SIV). The virus jumped species from simians to *Homo sapiens* through bushmeat and other improper interaction. In typical viral fashion, HIV mutated and spread from person to person. When it first breaks the species barrier, a virus has more spreading and killing power.

Eventually, the species can develop increased resistance, also known as herd immunity. Employing friendly organisms, like local honey fighting allergies, help some members of the herd. The human being's innate immune system contains monocytes, which can digest and kill harmful pathogens. The immune system's adaptive lymphocytes go to work protecting the body from more aggressive agents. Lymphocytes have memory; hence, those who recover from diseases like varicella virus / chicken pox become immune. Now and again, COVID-19 is a game changer.

America's first coronavirus case was documented on January 21, 2020, in Washington state. Mind you, that was the first *documented* case—much has slipped into America without documentation. We employ doors, locks, fences, and other security implements to protect against corporeal intruders. How do we protect against microbiological intruders? (Take a moment to brainstorm.)

Hunters and dogs, _beware_!

1. Anaplasmosis
2. Avian influenza
3. Babesiosis
4. Brucellosis
5. Campylobacter jejuni
6. Chronic wasting disease
7. Cryptosporidiosis
8. Deer parapoxvirus
9. Echinococcosis
10. Ehrlichiosis
11. Escherichia coli
12. Giardiasis
13. Hantavirus
14. Leptospirosis
15. Lyme borreliosis
16. Rabies
17. Rocky Mountain spotted fever
18. Salmonellosis/salmonella (a.k.a. food poisoning)
19. Toxoplasmosis
20. Trichinellosis
21. Tuberculosis

PART V

what now and How?

The same ammunition, which won the Revolutionary War, will protect us from microbiological intruders—our *spacious skies*, *purple mountains*, *woods and templed hills*[6], and every inch of our *heav'n rescued land*.[7] Life began in the Garden of Eden; therefore, humanity can only be redeemed through the garden by reconciling with nature. The land is our home, and we are all responsible caretakers. We are its parents and children. If dismissing good practices invited coronavirus to imprison human civilization in 2020, then reinstating good practices can combat it.

The American spirit is resilient and can turn a negative into a positive. We can confirm positive changes by honoring our traditional motto, "**E pluribus unum**," translated as "**Out of** *[E]* **many** *[pluribus]* **one** *[unum]*," meaning although Americans originate from many different races, religions, and cultures, we pledge as *one nation under God indivisible*. Stoicism of united souls confirmed in self-control are our most important ammunition against harm of any sort.

How America behaves during crises such as COVID-19 is critical to our success and status. People in powerful positions have disappointed millions of Americans who believed in them; however, we can *see beyond* and reclaim our original *patriot dreams*. Although negative socio-economic effects have thrown our fragmented society into disarray and widened the chasms, every American has the power to right such wrongs. Retracing our steps, we find the way back to reclaiming

---

6   Second verse of My Country, 'tis of Thee by Samuel Francis Smith.
7   Fourth verse of The Star-Spangled Banner.

our true identity as a world leader. Path to wellness means taking back control, armed with positive practices to build a cleaner, healthier future.

The most advanced nation with the highest standard of living on planet Earth has the ability to find the solution to the COVID-19 challenge in one, two, three. First make a list of positives like good, healthy habits and practices to reestablish. Second, make another list of negatives like bad habits and malpractices. The third step is making a list of alternatives by brainstorming new ideas or antidotes for each malpractice. Good practices will once again set us free.

First list. The positive states of America are as follows:

1. Good civic sense.
2. Freedom.
3. Garden clubs, rotary clubs, and numerous other civic organizations.
4. Equal opportunity.
5. Every citizen can participate in the government.
6. Volunteerism.
7. United we stand.
8. Constitution.
9. Do not litter.
10. Do not loiter.
11. Do not eliminate in public.
12. Idealism.
13. Vast arable lands.
14. Family farmstead.
15. Community gardens.
16. Public botanical gardens, parks, and libraries.
17. Botanical garden programs.[8]
    a. Tai Chi / wellness
    b. Food workshops (e.g., *Fresh Plates* and *Plant. Eat. Repeat.*)
    c. Art (e.g., mosaiculture)
    d. STEM (e.g., SlothBot[9])
    e. Beekeeping

---

8 Classes offered at Atlanta Botanical Garden.
9 A robot that collects data on pollinators, flowers, temperature, and humidity, created in partnership of Georgia Institute of Technology engineers and Atlanta Botanical Garden.

    f.   Habitats / ecological study

    g.   Constructing birdhouses and bat houses

18. Library programs.
    a.   Public computers
    b.   Free Wi-Fi
    c.   Free ESL[10] classes / literacy
    d.   Job fairs
    e.   Training classes
    f.   Story times
    g.   Book clubs

19. Protected lands / wildlife reserves.
20. Recycling / repurposing / Recology.[11]
21. Organic gardens / WWOOF.[12]
22. Remodeling / improving.
23. Goal oriented.
24. Always striving toward a more perfect union.
25. Open to changes / amendments.
26. Melting pot of cultures contributing new ideas.
27. Imagination, invention, and innovation.
28. Attracting new ideas, talents, and brains from overseas.
29. Seeking new ideas.
30. Accepting new ideas.

---

10 Abbreviation for English as a second language.
11 Organization devoted to zero-waste with locations in Washington, Oregon, and California.
12 Organization promoting sustainability, World Wide Opportunities on Organic Farms.

31. Making the best of bad situations and turning negatives into positives.
    a. Social distancing does not equal social isolation by accepting the namaste[13] greeting into our famous melting pot.
    b. Remote working and learning have allowed families more time together.
    c. Remote working and learning lowers traffic pollution which improves air quality.
    d. See neighbors more often.
    e. People spending more time at home deters burglars.

32. Please add your ideas to the positives list.

_____

_____

_____

_____

_____

_____

_____

_____

_____

_____

13 For further information, please read "Healthy Salutations" by D. J. Chakraborty.

Second list. Negatives requiring change are as follows:

1. Widespread panic / pandemonium.
2. Social mistrust.
3. Abusing a scapegoat.
4. Hoarding necessary supplies (e.g., toilet paper).
5. Hoarding currency.
6. Economic disruption.
7. Work stoppage.
8. Stock market collapse.
9. Increase in crime.
10. Linguistic segregation.
11. Racial inequality.
12. Neo-slavery.
13. Corpses stored in freezer trucks and/or shipped across country.
14. Spreading disease.
15. Landfills breeding leachate and other harmful matter.
16. Harmful pollutants (e.g., herbicides, pesticides, traffic, industry).
17. Invasive exotics disrupting ecosystem.
18. Unnecessary relocation.
19. Destroying verdure for development.
20. Abandoned, dilapidated real estate.
21. Invasiveness of Third World, Communists, theocracies, and penal colonies.
22. Overpopulation.
23. Fragmented society.
24. Theft of America's national identity.
25. Greed.
26. Obdurateness.
27. Corruption.
28. Please add your ideas to the negatives list.

Third list. Applying our positive characteristics, we find an extensive list of ways and means to cleanse each negative out of our homeland. In the words of President Bill Clinton, *"There is nothing wrong with America that cannot be cured by what is right with America."* **The alternatives are as follows:**

1. Bring community gardens to every neighborhood especially for low-income areas supervised by local garden club volunteers (e.g., the Giving Garden in Mableton, Georgia).
2. Cremate the dead.
3. Detritivores for waste management.
4. Coprovores for sewage management.
5. Permaculture.
6. Environmental stewardship.
7. Land ethic.
8. Institute community ESL instruction in every locale.
9. Use the namaste greeting.
10. Bioremediation.
11. Vermiculture.
12. Mycology.
13. Increase solar, wind, renewable energy.
14. Increase alternative fuel vehicles.
15. Increase remote activities (e.g., shopping, working).
16. Increase Recology.
17. Increase organic gardens / WWOOF.
18. Remodel / repurpose old dwellings over new construction.
19. Address and remedy global chemistry variance.
20. Address and remedy surface temperature variance.
21. Create more SlothBots to analyze global chemistry and surface temperature.

22. Money may not grow on trees, but investments do. One mature[14] tree provides enough oxygen for two human beings to breathe their entire lives. Some people practice the custom of planting two trees when a baby is born, investing in oxygen for their child, the child's future spouse, and two future grandchildren. Two trees of a species are needed for cross-pollination and planting in odd numbers increases aesthetic appeal.

    a.   Count the number of people in your home, school, or town.

    b.   Count the number of trees in the same locale.

    c.   Plant three (or required number) of native[15] trees in needy areas.

23. Control population by reducing numbers, like China's one-offspring mandate

    2020 = 7.8 billion (one-hundred-year life span)

    2121 = 3.9 billion like c. 1973

    2222 = 1.95 billion like c. 1929

    2323 = 975 million like c. 1700 (three hundred years to be under one billion)

24. Control population by finding a comfortable, uninhabited exoplanet to settle (create WarpBots[16] to explore).

25. Control population by building a space station/bubble on Mars.

26. Spontaneous volunteerism.

    (Anecdotal example: One day at the local grocery store, the author witnessed another customer coughing and sneezing on the self-scanner. That other customer wore no mask or gloves, also probed her orifices, touched the keypad, etc. Unconcerned, she walked out

---

14 Measuring about twelve-inch caliper, varies by species.

15 Look up by zip code in the National Audubon Society, National Wildlife Federation, Arbor Day Foundation websites.

16 Fast-moving version of SlothBots.

with her purchases. Two customers standing in the line refused to use that contaminated station. Furthermore, the grocery store was short-staffed; hence, the store employees did not have time to clean it.

The author was wearing her mask and gloves and asked a store cashier if she could borrow the cleaner and paper towels. The author thoroughly cleaned the entire station, including the scanner, screen, keypad, bag dispenser, etc. She then returned the cleaner and paper towels to the cashier, disposed of her old gloves, and put on a new pair. Finally, she scanned her groceries, paid, retrieved her receipt, and sanitized the station.

While the author was putting the receipt in her purse, a store employee and several customers said, "Ma'am, you are amazing,"

"That is the cleanest it's ever been,"

"Thank you for doing that, ma'am, I couldn't believe the other lady,"

"You are the best."

"I wish there were more people like you,"

"Would you come to my house?"

"You should be on the news!"

27.   Disarm viral villains (like example #26)
28.   Please add your ideas to the alternatives list.

PART VI

Testing

A. If negative, follow path A.
　　1. Social distancing
　　2. Safety precautions

B. If positive, follow path B.
　　1. Central quarantine isolation for treatment
　　2. Contact tracing

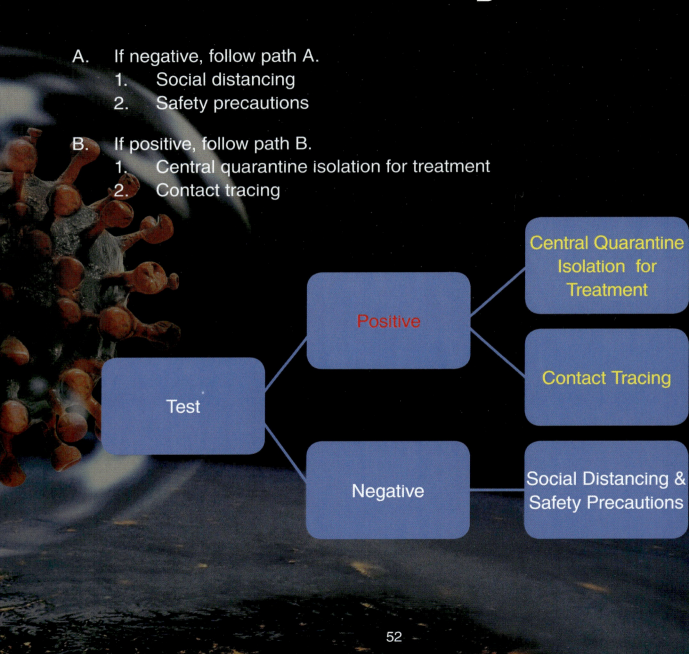

PART VII

YOU KNOW HOW

A. Technique for Washing Hands

1. Wet hands with clean running water.
2. Turn off faucet and lather with a disinfectant soap.
    a. Lather hands by rubbing them with soap. Lather the whole hand the backs, the palm, between fingers, and under finger-nails.
    b. For problematic, stubborn dirt, soak hands in a vessel of soapy water and scrub using a nail-brush or lemon slice.
3. Scrub hands for at least twenty (20) seconds. It should look as if hands are clad in soapy gloves up to the wrists or elbows if necessary.
4. Rinse hands clean under running water.
5. Dry hands with a clean towel or air dryer.
6. Moisturize hands with lotion.
7. Use sanitizer only temporarily when soap and water are not available. Wash ASAP. Sanitizer is a temporary remedy, not a substitute for proper handwashing, because surfactant properties work best to kill viruses.

Occasions required to wash hands are listed below. Common sense dictates not to touch face, hair, cell phone, etc. prior to handwashing!

1. After using the bathroom.
2. After doing dirty work (e.g., cleaning, gardening, scooping dog/cat excrement, taking out the garbage).
3. Before and after handling food (e.g., eating meals, cooking, serving).
4. After blowing nose, sneezing, coughing, etc.
5. Upon returning home after school, work, activities, etc.
6. Showering is best following certain situations / activities (see technique below).
7. Can you name more?

_____
_____
_____
_____
_____
_____
_____
_____
_____
_____
_____
_____
_____
_____
_____

B. Technique for brushing teeth

1. Use quality toothbrush.
   a. Power or manual is a personal preference, and anything with the American Dental Association (ADA) seal of approval is good.
   b. Soft bristles are more flexible to get around teeth and under gumline. Hard bristles wear enamel down.
   c. Change every three (3) months.
2. Use toothpaste with ADA seal of approval.
3. Upper jaw
   a. Brush gently in circles from gum to tooth; do not scrub like cleaning the bathroom because abrasive scrubbing damages enamel.
   b. Start from back left to front to back right, drawing a circle on the outside of each tooth.
   c. Move toothbrush behind and repeat meticulously, brushing from right to left behind the upper teeth in circular motion.
4. Brush the upper chewing surfaces.
5. Gently brush the palate/roof of your mouth.
6. Lower jaw
   a. Use the same gentle, circular motion on your lower jaw.
   b. Start from back right to front to back left, drawing a circle on the outside of each tooth.
   c. Move toothbrush behind and repeat, brushing from left to right behind the lower teeth in circular motion.
7. Brush the lower chewing surfaces.
8. Gently brush the tongue.
9. Rinse well.
10 Floss up to the gumline between upper teeth

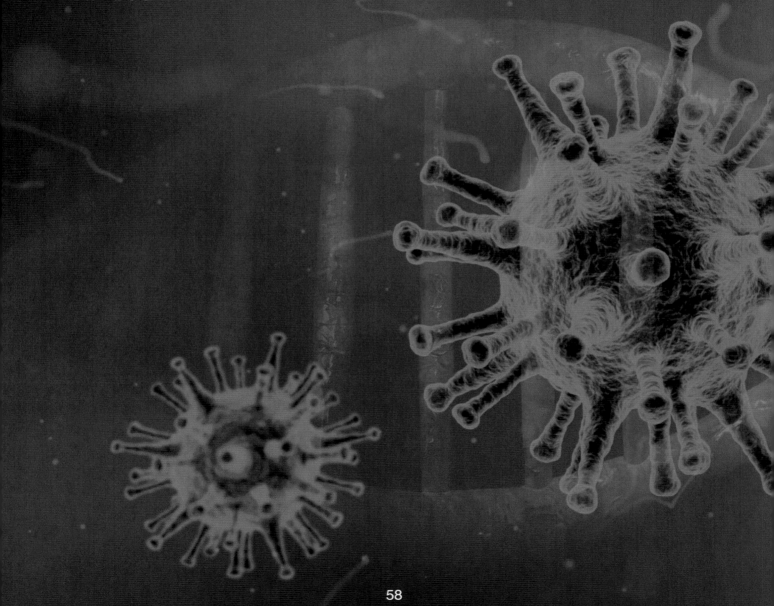

11. Floss down to the gumline between lower teeth.
12. Rinse well again.
13. Gargle with mouthwash or salt water.
14. Do a final rinse.

C. Technique for Digestive Cleansing

Consuming healthy foods and healing herbs will keep the body clean and free of diseases. A diet and herbal supplements with anti-inflammatory properties and rich in anti-oxidants yield a healthy physique. Drinking plenty of water is vital to good health. Furthermore, those benefits will build strength to fight off sickness, such as coronavirus. Researching the healing properties of herbs will provide additional information.

1. Green tea flushes toxins out of the system and provides multiple health benefits.
2. Tulsi (tea or vitamin supplement) has scientifically proven phytochemicals supporting every system of the body, even shown to prevent cancer.
3. Turmeric (food, tea, or vitamin supplement) is another whole-body benefactor.
4. Ginger (food, tea, or vitamin supplement) is another whole-body benefactor.
5. Can you name some more?

_____
_____
_____
_____
_____
_____
_____
_____

D. <u>Technique for Showering</u>

1. Wet head to toe with clean, hot running water to rinse off initial dust, grime, and sweat, also relaxing muscles. Quickly touch massage, making sure the entire body and hair are totally soaked.
2. Wash hair with shampoo. Start by thoroughly massaging scalp and continue to the end of each strand. Then repeat in reverse to rinse shampoo out. Rinse again until hair is clear of residue.
3. Conditioner is needed to moisturize hair as shampoo is to clean. Massage conditioner from ends to root, but not on scalp. Put on a plastic cap if necessary, according to label instructions.
4. Turn off water.
5. Massage face with facial soap. Start from the neck and work up to forehead. Draw circles on your skin using your fingers or a facial washcloth.
6. Clean orifices.
   a. *Eyes.* Close and gently soap lids.
   b. *Nose.* Gently soap outside, trim/tweeze nose hairs after shower, and use Navage[17] to cleanse sinus if required.
   c. *Mouth.* Close and gently soap lips and brush teeth (see technique above).
   d. *Ears.* Gently soap outside, trim/tweeze ear hairs after shower, and use hydrogen peroxide to cleanse canal if required.
7. Turn on water to rinse face clean, especially eyes, to avoid irritation.
8. Turn off water.
9. Massage entire body with body soap. Start from the neck and work down dorsal, ventral, arms, legs, feet, and between toes. Again draw

---

17 Nasal irrigation device.

circles on your skin using your fingers, a body washcloth, body sponge, or loofah. Remove conditioner cap if using.

10. Clean private parts and bottom orifice well.

    a. Practice proper toileting hygiene prior to showering and use moist cleansing cloths if unable to shower immediately.

    b. Install a Japanese toilet for optimum clean.

11. Turn on water to rinse clean. Meticulously touch massage again, making sure the entire body and hair are totally rinsed.

12. Tap dry with a clean towel.

13. Wrap long hair in a separate hair towel.

14. Moisturize face and body with emollient lotion.

15. Wear clean clothes.

16. Brush/comb/style hair as desired.

E. <u>Technique for Laundry</u>

1. Wash clothes (outerwear and underwear) worn eight (8) hours.
2. Change clothing (outerwear and underwear) every eight (8) hours.
   a. *Morning.* Cleanse, put on school/work attire, and place sleepwear in laundry.
   b. *Afternoon/evening.* (Home from school/work) Cleanse, put on house outfit, and place school/work attire in laundry.
   c. *Bedtime.* Cleanse, put on sleepwear, and place house outfit in laundry. If worn for less than eight hours, then hang up house outfit in an open space with good air circulation and wear it again.
3. Wash/change towels every other day.
4. Wash/change bedding every other week.

F.   <u>Technique for Cleaning House</u>

1.   Dust from top to bottom, starting with ceiling fixtures and crown molding and continuing to the floor.
2.   Dust all furniture and surfaces thoroughly with suitable cleaning agents.
3.   Sweep/vacuum floors, carpets, mats.
4.   Shake mats and area rugs outside to avoid redistributing dirt inside your home.
5.   Empty vacuum receptacles outside to avoid redistributing dirt inside your home.
6.   Clean kitchen thoroughly with suitable cleaning agents.
7.   Clean bathrooms thoroughly with suitable cleaning agents.
8.   Install screens on windows to safeguard your home from dust, pollen, and bugs.
9.   Install a screen door.
10.   Install sanitizing/HEPA (high efficiency particulate air) filters to safeguard your home from airborne pollutants.
11.   Remove outside shoes in garage or entranceway to avoid tracking dirt, dung, and other pollutants inside your home.
12.   Don a pair of inside shoes or house slippers to keep your feet clean and protected.

PART VIII

you. that's who

A. Did *you* find some interesting *glossary* words?

1. Are they *new*? Create your own symbol for *new*.

    Example: "Ṉň" or ✹

Word	Meaning	Code(s)
Example: Virus	A microscopic agent that produces disease in its host	

2.   Do some words *look* special on the page? Create symbol for *look*.

Example: "ᘭ" or ∞

Word	Meaning	Code(s)
Example: Arable	Lush (land), suitable for growing crops	∞

3. Are certain words fun to *say*? Create symbol for *say*.

   Example: "*Ss*" or

Word	Meaning	Code(s)
Example: Flummox	To puzzle (someone), bewilder, confuse, baffle, confound	

4. Are some words fun to *hear*? Create symbol for *hear*.

Example: "*Hh*" or Œ

Word	Meaning	Code(s)
Example: Bellicose	Ill-tempered and looking for a fight, hostile, warlike	Œ

Do some words fall into some other category? Consider some more categories and make up symbols for each and code your vocabulary. Do you think certain words fall into more than one category?

Word	Meaning	Code(s)
E x a m p l e : Inviolate	Safe from injury or violation, pure, unspoiled	Œ

B.   Do *you* have some interesting thoughts and ideas?

1.   Make technique posters to decorate your bathroom, laundry room, etc.
2.   Have you ever been sick with a virus?
3.   How did you feel?
4.   Has anyone in your family or a close friend ever been sick with a virus?
5.   How did that affect you?
6.   What are some bad habits that damage individual health?
7.   What are some bad practices that damage world health?
8.   How do you calm down when you are upset?
9.   How do you comfort family/friends when they are upset?
10. Can you name more changes or additions?
11. Can you think of ways to unite and act positively to help people you know?
     a.   Your family
     b.   Your school
     c.   Your neighborhood
     d.   Your (sports)team
     e.   Friends in need
     f.   Religious or civic organization
12. What are your ideas to improve/clean/decontaminate some troubled areas in your home-town?
13. Create a virtual presence device (e.g., seen on the television show The Big Bang Theory, season 4, episode 2, first aired on September 30, 2010).
14. Create a social distancing device (e.g., football helmet with face shield and bumper ball innovated by the author).
15. Perform a dramatic reading of "The Pandemic Limericks" individually or with your family/friends via social media and share with other family/friends via social media.

16. Choose your favorite pandemic limerick or limericks and expand to a one-act play and perform it individually or with your family/friends via social media and share with other family/friends via social media.

17. Set your favorite pandemic limerick or limericks to music and perform individually or with your family/friends via social media and share with other family/friends via social media. (e.g., "Alive" by the author please see pages 76-78).

18. Write your own song or adapt a favorite. Perform it individually or with your family/friends via social media and share with other family/friends via social media. (e.g., "Goodbye, Corona!" by the author which you sing to the tune of 1979 hit "My Sharona," please see pages 79-80).

19. Draw your image of Cyrus the Virus, Agent Greed, and other viral villains also create your own from your personal observations.

20. Draw some pictures of heroes like Aldo Leopold, Henrietta Lacks, and other forces of good nature, also create your own from your personal observations

21. Use recycled materials (e.g., plastic, glass, cardboard, magazines newspapers) to create architypes of your pictures.

22. Use recycled materials (e.g., plastic, glass, cardboard, magazines newspapers) to create a model of a city inside a space station/bubble or Mars including a safe avenue of ingress and egress.

23. Please list your ideas for social distancing sociably.

Alive

D.J. Chakraborty

Alive

(B18) Goodbye, Corona!

(Sing to the tune of the 1979 hit "My Sharona")

Ooh, you micro viral one, viral one,
    You know you are gonna be done, Corona.
    We are gonna be movin' on, movin' on.
    Time is gonna make us strong, Corona.

Never going to stop, give it up, 'till we're feeling well.
Never doubt, we're going to weed you out, send you back to hell.
    G-g-g-g-g-goodbye-aye. Whoa!
    G-g-g-g-goodbye, Corona.

Some bad moves made you come alive, come alive.
    We are going to find a vaccine, Corona.
    To find a cure, we're gonna strive, gonna strive.
    We are gonna wipe you clean, Corona.

Never going to stop, give it up, 'till we're feeling well.
Never doubt, we're going to weed you out, send you back to hell.
    G-g-g-g-g-goodbye-aye. Whoa!
    G-g-g-g-goodbye, Corona.

We are gonna wash our hands, sustain our land.
   It is just a matter of clime, Corona!
   It is d-d-destiny, manifest destiny,
   A strategic state of mind, Corona!

Never going to stop, give it up, 'till we're feeling well.
Never doubt, we're going to weed you out, send you back to hell.
   G-g-g-g-g-goodbye-aye. Whoa!
   G-g-g-g-goodbye, Corona.

Never going to stop, give it up, 'till we're feeling well.
Never doubt, we're going to weed you out, send you back to hell.
   G-g-g-g-g-goodbye-aye. Whoa!
   G-g-g-g-goodbye, Corona.

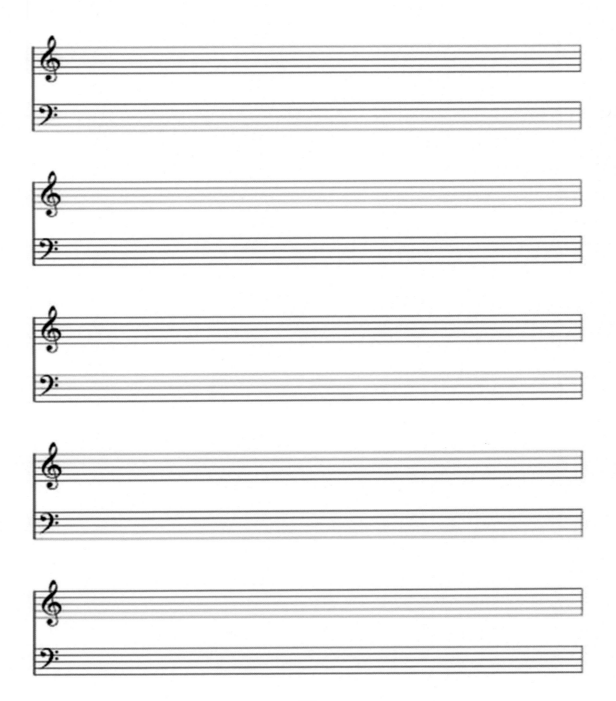

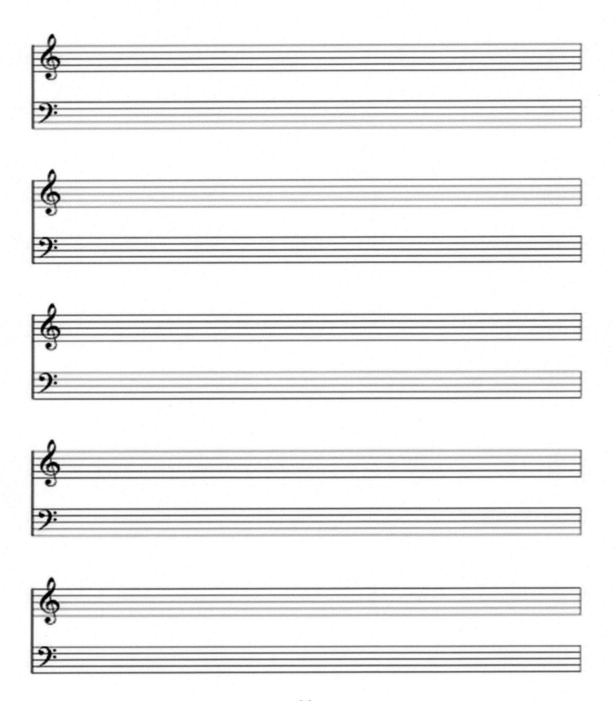

Abridged References

Bartoletti, Susan Campbell. *Terrible Typhoid Mary: A True Story of the Deadliest Cook in America*. Boston, MA: Houghton Mifflin Harcourt Publishing Company, 2015.

Birnbaum, Cara. *Universal Beauty*. Nashville, TN: Rutledge Hill Press, 2006.

Brown, Claude and K. Kirkman. *Trees of Georgia and Adjacent States*. Portland, OR: Timber Press, 1990.

Chakraborty, D. J. "Healthy Salutations." In *The Bright Side*,12. Smyrna, May 2020.

Chaplin, Lois Trigg. *The Southern Gardeners Book of Lists*. Lanham, MD: Taylor Trade Publishing, 1994.

Ferber, Linda S. *The Hudson River School: Nature and the American Vision*. New York Historical Society: Skira Rizzoli, 2009.

Leopold, Aldo. *For the Health of the Land*. Washington, DC: Island Press, 1999.

Pearl, Norman. *The Bald Eagle*. Minneapolis, MN: Picture Window Books, 2007.

Samuels, Tina M. *A Georgia Native Plant Guide*. Atlanta, GA: Mercer University Press, 2005.

Sherr, Lynn. *America the Beautiful: The Stirring True Story behind Our Nation's Favorite Song*. Cambridge, MA: The Perseus Books Group, 2001.

Skloot, Rebecca. *The Immortal Life of Henrietta Lacks*. New York, NY: Random House, 2010.

Snedden, Robert. *A World of Microorganisms*. New York: Scholastic Inc., 1996.

Steele, Philip. *Pandemics*. Chicago, IL: World Book Inc., 2008.

Wulf, Andrea. *Founding Gardeners*. New York, NY: Random House, 2011.

Printed in the United States
by Baker & Taylor Publisher Services